THE
WHISPERING MUMMY

By

SAX ROHMER

First published in 1918

This edition published by Read Books Ltd.
Copyright © 2019 Read Books Ltd.
This book is copyright and may not be
reproduced or copied in any way without
the express permission of the publisher in writing

British Library Cataloguing-in-Publication Data
A catalogue record for this book is available
from the British Library

CONTENTS

SAX ROHMER

Sax Rohmer was born in Ladywood, Birmingham, England in 1883. Hailing from a working class family, Rohmer briefly pursued careers in civil service and the theatre before turning to writing. In 1903, his first published work, 'The Mysterious Mummy', appeared in *Pearson's Weekly*. Rohmer continued to write weird fiction, and his major breakthrough came in 1912, when the first Fu-Manchu novel, *The Mystery of Dr. Fu-Manchu*, was serialized over a period of eight months. Rohmer's story of Fu-Manchu – an evil genius described as "the yellow peril incarnate in one man" – played off the imagined threat of Asian immigrants which was common in that day, and was an instant bestseller. Fu-Manchu went on to star in thirteen more novels, and – combined with his more conventional detective fiction – made Rohmer one of the most successful and well-paid authors of his day. Rohmer was a prolific writer right up to his death, which came as a result of an outbreak of Asian Flu.

THE
WHISPERING MUMMY

I

FELIX BRÉTON and I were the only occupants of the raised platform at the end of the hall; and the inartistic performance of the bulky dancer who occupied the stage promised to be interminable. From motives of sheer boredom I studied the details of her dress—a white dress, fitting like a vest from shoulder to hip, and having short, full sleeves under which was a sort of blue gauze. Her hair, wrists, and ankles glittered with barbaric jewelery and strings of little coins.

A deafening orchestra consisting of tambourines, shrieking Arab viols, and the inevitable *daràbukeh*, surrounded the performer in a half-circle; and three other large-sized *ghawâzi* mingled their shrill voices with the barbaric discords of the musicians. I yawned.

"As a quest of local color, Bréton," I said, "this evening's expedition can only be voted a dismal failure."

Felix Bréton turned to me, with a smile, resting his elbows upon the dirty little marble-topped table. He looked sufficiently like an artist to have been merely a painter; yet his gruesome picture "Le Roi S'Amuse" had proved the salvation of the previous Salon.

"Have patience," he said; "it is Shejeret ed-Durr (Tree of

7

Pearls) that we have come to see, and she has not yet appeared."

"Unless she appears shortly," I replied, stifling another yawn, "I shall disappear."

But even as I spoke, there arose a hum of excitement throughout the crowded room; the fat dancer, breathless from her unpleasing exertions, resumed her seat; and all the performers turned their heads towards a door at the side of the stage. A veiled figure entered, with slow, lithe step; and her appearance was acclaimed excitedly. Coming to the centre of the stage, she threw off her veil with a swift movement, and confronted the audience, a slim, barbaric figure. I glanced at Felix Bréton. His eyes were glittering with excitement. Here at last was the *ghazîyeh* of romance, the *ghazîyeh* of the Egyptian monuments; a true daughter of that mysterious tribe who, in the remote past of the Nile-land, wove spells of subtle moon-magic before the golden Pharaoh.

A monstrous crash from the musicians opened the music of the dance—the famous Gazelle dance—which commenced to a measure of long, monotonous cadences. Shejeret ed-Durr began slowly to move her arms and body in that indescribable manner which, like the stirring of palm fronds, speaks the veritable language of the voluptuous Orient. The attendant dancers clashing their miniature cymbals, the measure quickened, and swift passion informed the languorous body, which magically be came transformed into that of a leaping nymph, a bacchante, a living illustration of Keats' wonder-words:

> "Like to a moving vintage, down they came,
> Crown'd with green leaves, and faces all aflame;
> All madly dancing through the pleasant valley,
> To scare thee, Melancholy!"

At the conclusion of her dance, Shejeret ed-Durr, resuming her veil, descended to the floor of the hall and passed from table to table, exchanging light badinage with those patrons known to her.

"Do you think you could induce her to come up here, Kernaby?" said Bréton excitedly; "she is simply the ideal model for my 'Danse Funébre.'"

"Any inducement other than our presence in this select part of the establishment," I replied, offering him a cigarette, "is unnecessary. She will present herself with all reasonable despatch."

Indeed, I had seen the dark eyes glance many times towards us, as we sat there in distinguished isolation; and, even as I spoke, the girl was ascending the steps, from whence she approached our table, smiling in friendly fashion. Bréton's surprise was rather amusing when she confidently seated herself, giving an order to the cross-eyed waiter in close attendance. It would be our privilege, of course, to pay the bill. Of its being a privilege, no one could doubt who had observed the envious glances cast in our direction by less favored patrons.

As Bréton spoke no Arabic, the task of interpreter devolved upon me; and I was carrying on quite mechanically when my attention was drawn to a peculiarly sinister-looking person seated alone at a table close beside the corner of the stage. I remembered having observed him address some remark to Shejeret ed-Durr, and having noted that she seemed to avoid him. Now, he was directing upon us a glare so electrically baleful that when I first detected it I was conscious of a sort of shock. The man was rather oddly dressed, wearing a black turban and a sort of loose robe not unlike the *burnûs* of the desert Arabs. I concluded that he belonged to some religious order, and that his bosom was inflamed with a hatred of a most murderous character towards myself, Felix Bréton, and the dancer.

I endeavored, without attracting the girl's notice to indicate to Bréton the presence of the Man of the Glare; but the artist was so engrossed in contemplation of Shejeret ed-Durr and kept me so busy interpreting, that I abandoned the attempt in despair. Having made his wishes evident to her, the girl readily consented to pose for him; and when next I glanced at the table near the stage, the Man of the Glare had disappeared.

What induced me to look towards the rear of the platform upon which we were seated I know not, unless I did so in obedience to a species of hypnotic suggestion; but something prompted me to glance over my shoulder. And, for the second time that night, I encountered the gaze of mysterious eyes. From a little square window these compelling eyes regarded me fixedly, and presently I distinguished the outline of a head surmounted by a white turban.

The second watcher was Abû Tabâh!

What business could have brought the mysterious *imám* to such a place was a problem beyond my powers of conjecture, but that he was silently directing me to depart with all speed I presently made out. Having signified, by a gesture, that I had grasped the purport of his message, I turned again to Bréton, who was struggling to carry on a conversation with Shejeret ed-Durr in his native French.

I experienced some difficulty in inducing him to leave, but my arguments finally prevailed, and we passed out into the dimly lighted street. About us in the darkness pipes wailed, and there was the dim throbbing of the eternal *darábukeh*. We were in that part of El-Wasr adjoining the notorious Square of the Fountain. Discordant woman voices filled the night, and strange figures flitted from the shadows into the light streaming from the open doorways. It was the centre of secret Cairo, the midnight city; and three paces from the door of the dance hall, a slim, black-robed figure suddenly appeared at my elbow, and the musical voice of Abû Tabâh spoke close to my ear:

"Be on the terrace of Shepheard's in half an hour."

The mysterious figure melted again into the shadows about us.

II

On the deserted hotel balcony, Abû Tabâh awaited me.

"It was indeed fortunate, Kernaby Pasha," he said, "that I observed you this evening."

"I am greatly obliged to you," I replied, "for watching over me with such paternal solicitude. May I inquire what danger I have incurred?"

I was angrily conscious of feeling like a schoolboy suffering reproof.

"A very great danger," Abû Tabâh assured me, his gentle, musical voice expressing real concern. "Ahmad es-Kebîr is the lover of the dancer called Shejeret ed-Durr, although she who is of the *ghawâzi*, of Keneh does not return his affections."

"Ahmad es-Kebîr?—do you refer to a malignant looking person in a black turban?" I inquired.

Abû Tabâh gravely inclined his head.

"He is one of the *Rifa'îyeh*, the Black *Darwîshes*. They practise strange rites and are by some accredited with supernatural powers. For you the danger is not so great as for your friend, who seemed to be speaking words of love to the *ghazîyeh*."

I laughed shortly.

"You are mistaken, Abû Tabâh," I replied; "his interest was not of the character which you suppose. He is an artist and merely desired the girl to pose for him."

Abû Tabâh shrugged his shoulders.

"She is an unveiled woman," he said contemptuously, "but love in the heart of such a one as Ahmad is a terrible passion, consuming the vitals and rendering whom it afflicts either a partaker of Paradise or as one of the evil *ginn*."

"In the particular case under consideration," I said, "it

would seem distinctly to have produced the latter and less agreeable symptoms."

"Let your friend step warily," advised Abû Tabâh; "for some who have aroused the enmity of the Black *Darwîshes* have met with strange ends, nor has it been possible to fix responsibility upon any member of the order."

"You think my poor friend, Felix Bréton, may be discovered some morning in an unpleasantly messy condition?"

"The Black *Darwîshes* do not employ the knife," answered Abû Tabâh; "they employ strange and more subtle weapons."

I stared hard at him in the darkness. I thought I knew my Cairo, but this sounded unpleasantly mysterious. However—

"I am indebted to you, Abû Tabâh," I said, "for your timely warning. As you know, I always personally avoid any possibility of misunderstanding in regard to my relations with Egyptian womenfolk."

"With some rare exceptions," agreed Abû Tabâh, "particulars of which escape my memory at the moment, you have always been a model of discretion, Kernaby Pasha."

"I will warn my friend," I said hastily, "of the view of his conduct mistakenly taken by the gentleman in the black turban."

"It is well," replied Abû Tabâh; "we shall meet again ere long."

With that and the customary dignified salutations he departed, leaving me wondering what hidden significance lay in his words, "we shall meet again ere long."

Experience had taught me that Abû Tabâh's warnings were not to be lightly dismissed, and I knew enough of the fanaticism of those strange Eastern sects whereof the *Rifa'îyeh*, or Black *Darwîshes*, was one, to realize that it would prove an unhealthy amusement to interfere with their domestic affairs. Felix Bréton, who possessed the rare gift of capturing and transferring to canvas the atmosphere of the East with the opulent colorings and vivid contrasts which constitute its charm, had nevertheless but little practical experience of the manners and customs of the golden Orient. He had leased a large studio situated on the roof of a fine old Cairene palace hidden away behind the Street of the Booksellers and almost in the shadow of the Mosque of el-Azhar. His romantic spirit had prompted him after a time to give up his rooms at the Continental and to take up his abode in the apartment adjoining the studio; that is to say, completely to cut himself off from European life and to become an inhabitant of the Oriental city. With his imperfect knowledge of the practical side of native life in the East, I did not envy him; but I was fully alive to his danger, isolated as he was from the European community, indeed from modernity; for out of the boulevards of modern Cairo into the streets of the *Arabian Nights* is but a step, yet a step that bridges the gulf of centuries.

As I entered his studio on the following morning, I discovered him at work upon the extraordinary picture "Danse Funébre." Shejeret ed-Durr was posing in the dress of an ancient priestess of Isis. Bréton briefly greeted me, waving his hand towards a cushioned *dîwan* before which stood a little coffee-table bearing decanters, siphons, cigarettes, and other companionable paraphernalia. Making myself comfortable, I studied the picture and the model.

"Danse Funébre" was an extraordinary conception, representing an elaborately furnished modern room, apparently that of an antiquary or Egyptologist; for a multitude of queer relics decorated the walls, cabinets, and the large table at which a man was seated. Boldly represented immediately to the left of his chair stood a mummy in an ornate sarcophagus, and forth from the swathed figure into the light cast downwards from an antique lamp, floated a beautiful spirit shape—that of an Egyptian priestess. Upon her face was an expression of intense anger, as, her fingers crooked in sinister fashion, she bent over the man at the table.

The mummy and sarcophagus depicted on the canvas stood before me against the wall of the studio, the lid resting beside the case. It was moulded, as is sometimes seen, to represent the face and figure of the occupant and was as fine an example of the kind as I had met with. The mummy was that of a priestess and dancer of the Great Temple at Philæ, and it had been lent by the museum authorities for the purpose of Bréton's picture.

His enthusiasm at first seeing Shejeret ed-Durr was explainable by the really uncanny resemblance which the girl bore to the modeled figure. Studying her, from my seat on the *dîwan*, as she posed in that gauzy raiment depicted upon the lid of the sarcophagus, it seemed indeed that the ancient priestess was reborn in the form of Shejeret ed-Durr the *ghazîyeh*. Bréton had evidently tabooed make-up, with the exception of the characteristic black bordering to the eyes (which appeared in the presentment of the servant of Isis); and seen now in its natural coloring the face of the dancing-girl had undoubted beauty.

Presently, whilst the model rested, I informed Bréton of my conversation with Abû Tabâh; but, as I had anticipated, he was sceptical to the point of derision.

"My dear Kernaby," he said, "is it likely that I am going to interrupt my work now that I have found such an inspiring model, because some ridiculous *darwîsh* disapproves?"

"It is highly unlikely," I admitted; "but do not make the mistake of treating the matter lightly. You are right off the map here, and Cairo is not Paris."

"It is a great deal safer!" he cried in his boisterous fashion, "and infinitely more interesting."

But my mind was far from easy; for in the dark eyes of the model, when their glance rested upon Felix Bréton, there was that to have aroused poisonous sentiments in the bosom of the Man of the Glare.

III

During the course of the following month I saw Felix Bréton two or three times, and he was enthusiastic about the progress of his picture and the beauty of his model. The first hint that I received of the strange idea which was to lead to stranger happenings came one afternoon when he had called upon me at Shepheard's.

"Do you believe in reincarnation, Kernaby?" he asked suddenly.

I stared at him in surprise.

"Regardless of my personal views on the matter," I replied, "in what way does the subject interest you?"

Momentarily he hesitated; then—

"The resemblance between Yâsmîna" (this was the real name of Shejeret ed-Durr) "and the priestess of Isis," he said, "appears to me too marked to be explainable by mere coincidence. If the mummy were my personal property I should unwrap it——"

"Do you seriously desire me to believe that you regard Yâsmîna as a reincarnation of the elder lady?"

"That or a lineal descendant," he answered. "The tribe of the *Ghawâzi* is of unknown antiquity and may very well be descended from those temple dancers of the days of the Pharaohs. If you have studied the ancient wall paintings, you cannot have failed to observe that the dancing girls represented have entirely different forms from those of any other women depicted and from those of the ordinary Egyptian women of to-day."

His enthusiasm was tremendous; he was one of those uncomfortable fanatics who will ride a theory to the death.

"I cannot say that I have noticed it," I replied. "Your knowledge of the female form divine is doubtless more extensive than mine."

"My dear Kernaby," he cried excitedly, "to the trained eye the difference is extraordinary. Until I saw Yâsmîna I had believed the peculiar form to which I refer to be extinct like the blue enamel and the sacred lotus. If it is not reincarnation it is heredity." I could not help thinking that it more closely resembled insanity than either; but since Bréton had made no reference to the wearer of the black turban, I experienced less anxiety respecting his physical than his mental welfare.

Three days later there was a dramatic development. Drifting idly into Bréton's studio one morning I found him pacing the place in despair and glaring at his unfinished canvas like a man distraught.

"Where is Shejeret ed-Durr?" I inquired.

"Gone!" he replied. "She disappeared yesterday and I can find no trace of her."

"Surely the excellent Suleyman, proprietor of the dancing establishment, can assist you?"

"I tell you," cried Bréton savagely, "that she has disappeared. No one knows what has become of her."

I looked at him in dismay. He presented a mournful spectacle. He was unshaven and his dark hair was wildly disordered. His despair was more acute than I should have supposed possible in the circumstances; and I concluded that his interest in Yâsmîna was deeper than I had assumed or that I was incapable of comprehending the artistic temperament. I suppose the Gallic blood in him had something to do with it, but I was unspeakably distressed to observe that the man was on the verge of tears.

Consolation was impossible, and I left him pacing his empty studio distractedly. That night at an unearthly hour, long after I had retired to my own apartments, he came to Shepheard's. Being shown into my room, and the servant having departed—

"Yâsmîna is dead!" he burst out, standing there, a disheveled figure, just within the doorway.

"What!" I exclaimed, standing up from the table at which I had been writing and confronting him. "Dead? Do you mean——"

"He has murdered her!" said Bréton, in a dull monotonous

voice—"that fiend of whom you warned me."

I was appalled; for I had been utterly unprepared for such a tragedy.

"Who discovered her?"

"No one discovered her; she will never be discovered! He has buried her body in some secret spot in the desert."

My amazement grew with every word that he uttered, and presently—

"Then how in Heaven's name did you learn of her murder?" I asked.

Felix Bréton, who had begun to pace up and down the room, a truly pitiable figure, paused and looked at me wildly.

"You will think that I am mad, Kernaby," he said; "but I must tell you—I must tell someone. I could see that you were incredulous when I spoke to you of reincarnation, but I was right, Kernaby, I was right! Either that or my reason is deserting me."

My opinion inclined distinctly in the direction of the latter theory, but I remained silent, watching Bréton's haggard face.

"To-night," he continued, "as I sat looking at my unfinished picture and trying to imagine what could have become of Yâsmîna, the mummy—the mummy of the priestess—*spoke to me!*"

I slowly sank back into my chair. I was now assured that Felix Bréton had formed a sudden and intense infatuation for Yâsmîna and that her mysterious disappearance had deranged his sensitive mind. Words failed me; I could think of nothing to say; and bending towards me his haggard face—

"It whispered to me," he said, "in *her* voice—in my own language, French, as I have taught it to her; just a few imperfect words, but sufficient to convey to me the story of the tragedy. Kernaby, what does it mean? Is it possible that her spirit, released from the body of Yâsmîna, has returned to that which I firmly believe it formerly inhabited?..."

I had had the misfortune to be a party to some distressing scenes, but few had affected me so unpleasantly as this. That poor Felix Bréton was raving I could not doubt, but having persuaded him to spend the night at Shepheard's and having seen him safely to bed, I returned to my own room to endeavor to work out the problem of what steps I should take regarding him on the morrow.

In the morning, however, he seemed more composed, having shaved and generally rendered himself more presentable; but the wild look still lingered in his eyes and I could see that the strange obsession had secured a firm hold upon him. He discussed the matter quite calmly during breakfast, and invited me to visit the scene of this supernatural happening. I assented, and hailing *arabîyeh* we drove together to the studio.

There was nothing abnormal in the appearance of the place, but I examined the mummy and the mummy case with a new curiosity; for if Felix Bréton was not mad (and this was a point upon which I recognized my incompetence to decide) the phantom voice was clearly the product of some trick. However, I was unable to discover anything to account for it. The sarcophagus stood against the outer wall of the studio and near to a large lattice window before which was draped a heavy tapestry curtain for the purpose of excluding undesirable light upon that side of the model's throne. There was no balcony outside the window, which was fully, thirty feet from the street below; therefore unless someone had been hiding in the window recess beside the sarcophagus, trickery appeared to be out of the question. Turning to Bréton, who was watching me haggardly—

"You searched the recess last night?" I said.

"I did—immediately. There was no one there. There was no one anywhere in the studio; and when I looked out of the open window, the street below was deserted from end to end."

Naturally, I took it for granted that he would avoid the place, at any rate by night; and I said as much, as we passed along the Mûski together. I can never forget the wildness in his eyes as he turned to me.

"I *must* go back, Kernaby," he said. "It seems like desertion, base and cowardly."

IV

Bréton did not join me at dinner that evening as we had arranged that he should do, and towards the hour of ten o'clock, growing more and more uneasy on his behalf, I set out for the studio, half hoping that I should meet him. I saw nothing of him, however, as I crossed the Ezbekîyeh Gardens and the Atabet el-Khadrâ into the Mûski. From thence onward to the Rondpoint the dark and narrow streets were almost deserted, and from the corner of the Shâria el-Khordâgîya to the Street of the Bookbinders I met with no living thing save a lean and furtive cat.

My footsteps echoed hollowly from wall to wall of the overhanging buildings, as I approached the door giving access to the courtyard from which a stair communicated with the studio above. The moonlight, slanting down into the ancient place, left more than half of it in densest shadow, but just touched the railing of the balcony and the lower part of the *mushrabîyeh* screen masking what once had been the *harêm* apartments from the view of one entering the courtyard. Far above me, through an open lattice, a dim light shone out, though vaguely. This part of the house was bathed in the radiance of the moon, which dimmed that of the studio lamp; for the open window was the window of Bréton's studio.

The door at the foot of the stairs was partly open, and I ascended slowly, since the place was quite dark and I was forced to feel my way around the eccentric turnings introduced by an Arab architect to whom simplicity had evidently been an abomination.

A modern door had been fitted to the studio; and although this door was also unfastened, I rapped loudly, but, receiving no answer, entered the studio. It was empty. The lamp was lighted, as I had observed from below, and a faint aroma of Turkish tobacco smoke hung in the air. Clearly, Bréton had left but a few moments earlier; and I judged it probable that he would be returning very shortly, for had he set out for Shepheard's he would not have left his door unlocked, and in any event I should have met him on the way. Therefore, having glanced into the inner room, which, latterly, Bréton had been using as a bedroom, I sat down on the *dîwan* and prepared to await his return.

The lamp whose light I had seen shining through the window was that which hung before the model's throne, and the curtain which usually draped the window recess had been partially pulled aside, so that from where I sat I could see part of the centre lattice, which was open. My mind at this time was entirely occupied with uneasy speculations regarding Bréton, and although I had glanced more than once at the large unfinished picture on the easel, from which the face of Shejeret ed-Durr peered out across the shoulder of the seated man, and several times had looked at the mummy set upright in its painted sarcophagus, no sense of the uncanny had touched me or in any way prepared me for the amazing manifestation which I was about to witness.

How long I had sat there I cannot say exactly; possibly for ten minutes or a quarter of an hour: when, suddenly, an eerie whisper crept through the stillness of the big room!

Since I had more than once been temporarily tricked into belief in the supernatural, by means of certain ingenious devices, I did not readily fall a victim to the mysterious nature of the present occurrence. Yet I must confess that my heart gave a great leap and I was forced to exert all my will to control my nerves. I sat quite still, listening intently for a repetition of that evil whisper. Then, in the stillness, it came again.

"Felix," it breathed, "because of you I lie dead in a grave in the desert.... I died for you, Felix, and now I am so lonely...."

The whispering voice offered no clue to the age or the sex of the speaker; for a true whisper is toneless. But the words, as

Bréton had declared, were uttered in broken French and spoken with a curious accent.

It ceased, that ghostly whispering; and I realized that my nerves could stand no more of it; for that it came or seemed to come from the mummy of the priestess was a fact as undeniable as it was horrible.

Resorting to action, I sprang up and leaped across the room, grasping first at the curtain draped in the window on the right of the sarcophagus. I jerked it fully aside. The recess was empty. All three lattices were open, on the right, left, and in the centre of the window; but, craning out from the latter, I saw the street below to be vacant from end to end.

Stepping back into the room, and metaphorically clutching my courage with both hands, I approached the sarcophagus, peered behind it, all around it, and, finally, into the swathed face of the mummy itself. Nothing rewarded my search. But the studio of Felix Bréton seemed to have become icily cold; at any rate I found myself to be shivering; and walking deliberately, although it cost me a monstrous effort to do so, I descended the dark winding stairway into the courtyard, and, on regaining the street, discovered to my intense annoyance that my brow was wet with cold perspiration.

I had taken no more than ten paces in the direction of the Sûk es-Sûdan when I heard the sound of approaching footsteps, and for some reason (I can only suppose as a result of my highly strung condition) I stepped into the shelter of a narrow gateway, where I could see without being seen, and there awaited the appearance of the one who approached.

It was Felix Bréton, his face showing ghastly in the moonlight as he turned the corner. I could not be certain if a mere echo had deceived me, but I thought I could detect faintly the softer footfalls of someone who was following him. From my cover I had an uninterrupted view of the entrance to the house which I had just left; and without showing myself I watched Bréton approach the door. At its threshold he seemed to hesitate; and in that brief hesitancy were illustrated the conflicting emotions driving the man. I recalled the words he had spoken to me that morning. "I must go back, Kernaby; it seems like desertion, base and cowardly." He opened the door and disappeared.

As he did so, a second figure crossed from the shadows on the opposite side of the street—that is, the side upon which I was concealed; and in turn advanced towards the door. As he passed my hiding-place I acted. Without an instant's hesitation I hurled myself upon him.

How he avoided that furious attack—if he did avoid it—or whether in the darkness I miscalculated my spring, I do not know to this day: I only know that I missed my objective, stumbled, recovered myself ... and turned with clenched fists to find *Abû Tabâh* confronting me!

"Kernaby Pasha!" he cried.

"Abû Tabâh!" said I dazedly.

"I perceive that I am not alone in my anxiety for the welfare of M. Felix Bréton."

"But why were you following him? I narrowly missed assaulting you."

"Very narrowly," he agreed in his gentle manner; "but you ask me why I was following M. Bréton. I was following him because I have seen so many of those who have crossed the path of the Black *Darwîshes* meet with violent and inexplicable deaths."

"Murder?" I whispered.

"Not murder—suicide. Therefore, observing, as I had anticipated, a strangeness in your friend's behavior, I have watched him."

"The strangeness of his behavior is easily accounted for," I said. And excitedly, for the horror of the episode in the studio was still strongly upon me, I told him of the whispering mummy.

"These are very dreadful things of which you speak, Kernaby Pasha," he admitted, "but I warned you that it was ill to incur the enmity of the Black *Darwîshes*. That there is a scheme afoot to compass the self-destruction or insanity of your friend is now evident to me; and he has brought this calamity upon himself; for the words which he believed to be spoken by the spirit of the girl Yâsmîna would not have affected him so unpleasantly if his attitude towards her had been marked by proper restraint and the affair confined within suitable limitations."

"Quite so. But although the Black *Darwîshes* may be both malignant and clever, that uncanny whispering is beyond the control of natural forces."

"Such is not my opinion," replied Abû Tabâh. "A spirit does not mistake one person for another; and the whispering voice addressed itself to 'Felix' when Felix was not present. I believe, Kernaby Pasha, that you are the possessor of a pair of excellent opera-glasses? May I suggest that you return to Shepheard's and procure them."

V

The platform of the minaret seemed very cold to the touch of my stockinged feet; for I had left my shoes at the entrance to the mosque below in accordance with custom; and now, from the wooden balcony, I overlooked the neighboring roofs of Cairo, and Abû Tabâh, beside me, pointed to where a vague patch of light broke the darkness beneath us to the left.

"The window of M. Felix Bréton's studio," he said.

Raising the glasses to his eyes, he gazed in that direction, whilst I also peered thither and succeeded in making out the well of the courtyard and the roofs of the buildings to right and left of it. It was not evident to me for what Abû Tabâh was looking, and when presently he lowered the glasses and turned to me I expressed my doubts in words.

"It is surely evident," I said, speaking, as I now almost invariably did to the *imám*, in English, of which he had a perfect mastery, "that we have little chance of discovering anything from here, since nothing was visible from the studio window. Furthermore, who save Yâsmîna could have spoken in the manner which I have related and in broken French?"

"An eavesdropper," he replied, "might have profited by the lessons which Yâsmîna received from M. Bréton; and all vocal characteristics are lost in a whisper. In the second place, Yâsmîna is not dead."

"What!" I cried.

Although, when Bréton had informed me of her death, I myself had doubted him, for some reason the ghostly whisper had convinced me as it had convinced him.

"She has been kept a prisoner during the past week in a house belonging to one of the Black *Darwîshes*," continued Abû Tabâh;

"but my agents succeeded in tracing her this morning. By my orders, however, she has not been allowed to return to her home."

"And what was the object of those orders?"

"That I might learn for what purpose she had been made to disappear," replied Abû Tabâh; "and I have learned it to-night."

"Then you think that the whispering mummy——"

He suddenly clutched my arm.

"Quick! raise your glasses!" he said softly. "On the roof of the house to the left of the light. There is the whispering mummy!"

Strung up to a high pitch of excitement, I gazed through the glasses in the direction indicated by my companion. Without difficulty I discerned him—a man wearing a black turban—who crept like some ungainly cat along the flat roof, carrying in his hand what looked like one of those sugar canes which pass for a delicacy among the natives, but which to European eyes appear more suitable for curtain-poles than sweetmeats. Springing perilously across a yawning gulf, the wearer of the black turban gained the roof of the studio, crept along for some little distance further, and then, lying prone, began slowly to lower the bamboo rod in the direction of the lighted window.

I found that unconsciously I had suspended my respiration, and now, breathlessly, as the truth came home to me—

"It is a speaking-tube!" I cried, "I cannot see the end of it, but no doubt it is curved so as to protrude through the side of the lattice window. Do you look, Abû Tabâh: I propose to act."

Thrusting the glasses into the *imám's* hand, I took my Colt repeater from my pocket, and, having peered for some seconds steadily in the direction of the dimly visible *Darwîsh*, I opened fire! I had fired five shots in the heat of my anger at that sinister crouching figure, ere Abû Tabâh seized my wrist.

"Stop!" he cried; "do you forget where you stand?"

Truly I had forgotten in my indignation, or I should not have outraged his feelings by firing from the minaret of a mosque. But sufficient of my wrath remained to occasion me a thrill of satisfaction, when, peering through the dusk, I saw the *Darwîsh* throw up his arms and disappear from view.

* * * * *

"There is blood in the courtyard," said Abû Tabâh; "but Ahmad es-Kebîr has fled. Therefore he still lives, and his anger will be not the less but the greater. Depart from Cairo, M. Bréton: it is my counsel to you."

"But," cried Felix Bréton, glaring wildly at the big canvas on the easel, "I must finish my picture. As Yâsmîna is alive, she must return, and I must finish my picture!"

"Yâsmîna cannot return," replied Abû Tabâh, fixing his weird eyes upon the speaker. "I have caused her to be banished from Cairo." He raised his hand, checking Bréton's hot words ere they were uttered. "Recriminations are unavailing. Her presence disturbs the peace of the city, and the peace of the city it is my duty to maintain."

Printed in Great Britain
by Amazon

16803355R00016